After packing a huge lunch, Dee and Magee set off in their boat for a relaxing day on the water. But what begins as a fun day in the sun turns into a bumpy ride, when one bored little whale swims up to give their boat a friendly nudge hello.

Chris Van Dusen's charming illustrations and silly, rhyming story will keep readers giggling 'til the end of Dee and Magee's most extraordinary ride.

"The gouache cartoons . . . are bright, comical, and alive with color and detail. . . . A strong debut for Van Dusen."
—*School Library Journal*

". . . one whale of a tale."
—*Publishers Weekly*

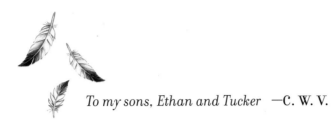

*To my sons, Ethan and Tucker* —C. W. V.

First paperback edition published in 2006 by Chronicle Books LLC.

Book design by Kristine Brogno.
Typeset in Filosophia.
The illustrations in this book were rendered in gouache.
**Manufactured in China**
ISBN 978-0-8118-5225-8

The Library of Congress has catalogued the previous edition as follows:
Van Dusen, Chris.
Down to the Sea with Mr. Magee / by Chris Van Dusen.
p. cm.
Summary: While spending the day in their boat on the sea,
Mr. Magee and his dog get caught up in wacky adventures
with a playful pod of whales.
ISBN 0-8118-2499-3
[1. Seashore—Fiction.
2. Whales—Fiction. 3. Stories in rhyme.] I. Title.
PZ8.3.V335 Do 2000
[E]—dc21
99-006879

20 19 18 17 16 15 14 13 12 11

Chronicle Books LLC
680 Second Street, San Francisco, California, 94107

www.chroniclekids.com

# Down
## to the
# Sea
## with
# Mr.
# Magee

by
Chris Van Dusen

chronicle books · san francisco

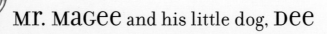Mr. Magee and his little dog, Dee

Loved spending time in their boat on the sea.

So early one morning at 6:32

They made a decision: that's just what they'd do.

Right after breakfast Magee packed a lunch:
Sandwiches, carrots, a thermos of punch,
    A big box of raisins, some sweet pickled beets,
Chocolate chip cookies and crunchy dog treats.
    With plans for the day and enough lunch for three,
They hopped in the car and drove down to the sea.

The pair left the dock at seven o'clock
And motored their way around Eagle Egg Rock.
They passed by the lighthouse and by the old wreck
With Magee at the wheel and Dee on the deck.

They suddenly spied off the bow to the east
A big pod of whales (there were fifty at least!)
Splashing about in the bright morning sun,
Feasting on shrimp and sardines by the ton.

But one little whale who had eaten his fill —

Munching on minnows and plankton and krill —

Was bored with his breakfast and since he was through,

He swam off in search of something to do.

Now Dee and Magee in their boat on the bay
Didn't notice the whale that was heading their way.
They were watching the other whales put on a show
And soon that young whale was directly below!

From under the sea the little whale spied
MAGEE and DEE'S boat — but not them inside.
He longed for adventure. He wanted to play.
So he bumped at the boat in a most friendly way.
Then the whale placed his blowhole directly below
And ever so gently he started to blow.

Magee saw the bubbles. He felt the boat sway.

Then up went the boat on a fountain of spray!

Higher and higher the little boat flew

As harder and harder that little whale blew.

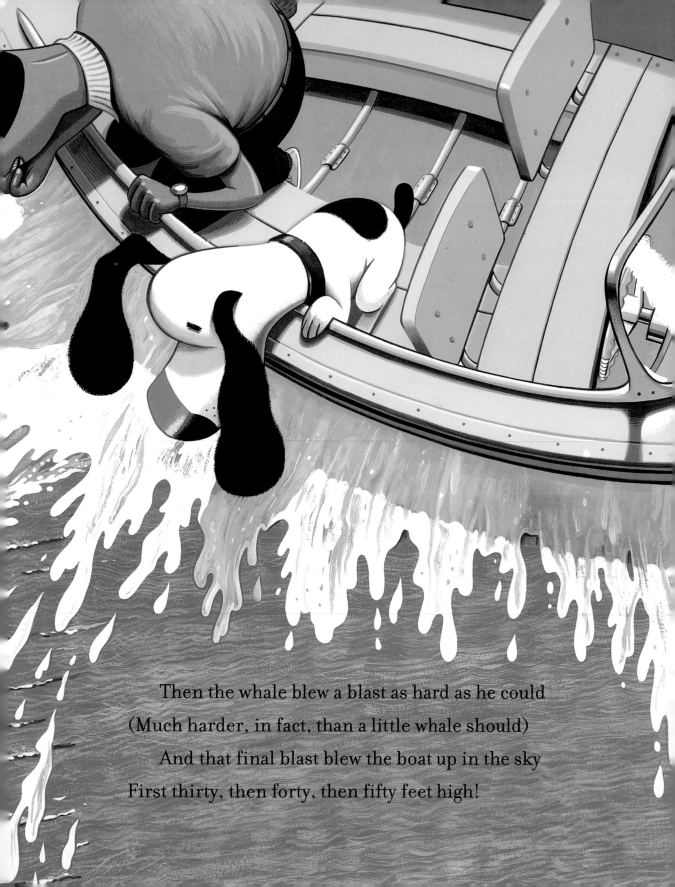

Then the whale blew a blast as hard as he could
(Much harder, in fact, than a little whale should)
And that final blast blew the boat up in the sky
First thirty, then forty, then fifty feet high!

The boat kept on rising, but it didn't stop there—
Wind hit it hard and it flew through the air.

DEE and MAGEE sailed over the sea
When all of a sudden...

They got stuck in a tree.

So there they were, stranded, MaGee and his pup,
In the top of a spruce, sixty-something feet up.

From their perch in the sky the two watched in dismay
As the whale far below swam swiftly away.

MaGee was downhearted. Just what could he do?
They seemed hopelessly stuck, but little Dee knew.
The secret to get the boat safely unpinned
Was to rock back and forth and wait for the wind.

So they rocked and they rocked for an hour or so,
But the boat didn't budge 'cause the wind didn't blow.
Just when they thought they'd be stuck there all night
They spotted, far off, a spectacular sight.

Away in the distance, across the blue bay
The whales — all fifty — were heading their way!
They swam through the water in one long, straight row
And gathered around the small island below.

Magee looked down at the circle of whales
Surrounding the island and raising their tails.
He felt a bit nervous, a little bit tense
When all of a sudden, it made perfect sense!
"They're trying to save us!" he shouted with glee.
"Hold on, Dee! Hold on! As tight as can be!"

Their tails slapped down with a thunderous crash

Which in turn created a super-high splash

That covered the island and raced up the tree

And dislodged the boat — and set them both free!

Dee was so happy she let out a yelp.
Magee tipped his hat to the whales for their help.
"Thank you, my friends, for saving the day."
Then they all waved goodbye and the whales swam away.

On the way home, little Dee had a thought:
What about all of the food they had brought?

In all the excitement, they ate not a bite…

So they saved it and had it for dinner that night.

CHRIS VAN DUSEN always wanted to paint a picture of a boat in the top of a tree. When he wrote a story around that idea, MR. MAGEE and DEE were born. CHRIS lives down by the sea in Maine, with his wife, two sons and, naturally, a dog.

**Also by Chris Van Dusen**

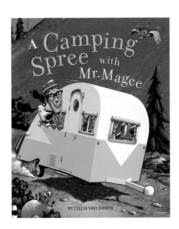